This igloo book belongs to:

........................................................................

# igloobooks

Published in 2019
by Igloo Books Ltd, Cottage Farm, Sywell, NN6 0BJ
www.igloobooks.com

Copyright © 2018 Igloo Books Ltd
Igloo Books is an imprint of Bonnier Books UK

GOL002 0419
2 4 6 8 10 9 7 5 3 1
ISBN 978-1-78670-872-4

Written by Stephanie Moss
Illustrated by Nina de Polonia-Nill

Cover designed by Kerri-Ann Hulme and Jason Shortland
Interiors designed by Jason Shortland
Edited by Caroline Richards

Printed and manufactured in China

Written by Stephanie Moss

Illustrated by Nina de Polonia-Nill

# The Very SMELLY ♛ Princess

igloobooks

There was a problem at the palace and it got worse every day.
The princess wouldn't have a bath, no matter what the queen would say.

At the sound of running water,
Princess Grace started to

# SCREAM!

Then she'd run off down the hall,
quick as the royal sprinting team.

The king bought her lots of toys and ran her baths with bubbles, too.

But she'd avoid the soapy water with the **naughty** tricks she knew.

After a little while of course, Princess Grace began to **smell.**
Her parents noticed first... then everyone else did, as well!

She **ponged** at royal processions.

Soldiers smelled her while on guard.

Grace's ponies all agreed she was the **stinkiest** in the yard.

Then there was the royal banquet.
**"This smells funny,"** one guest said.

As Grace left the table, the queen's cheeks turned **crimson** red.

"That's it!" declared the king.
"I'm sending out a royal decree."

"Whoever solves this problem can have
**jewels** and **gold** from me!"

Soon there was a line of people, all hoping to try their luck.
Some came with **strange** inventions. One had a **giant** rubber duck!

First, pop star Tilly Twinkles gave Grace tickets to her show.

**TICKET**

When Grace knew she'd have to wash, the **smelly** princess just said, **"No!"**

Her Fairy Godmother arrived and said, **"I'll fix this with one spell!"**

But she disappeared at once because she couldn't stand the smell.

Some pirates whispered their advice. **"Just wash behind your ears!"** But it was clear to the princess they hadn't washed in several years.

By the end of the day, everyone's patience had worn thin.
The queen pointed at the bath, and she shouted...

"JUST GET IN!"

Grace thought of the last few days. She felt so angry, she might **cry!**
She **still** didn't want a bath, but Mum needed to know why.

"Mummy," began Grace, "I'm a princess. Yes, that's true...

... but I **don't** like wearing fancy dresses every day, like you."

Grace liked playing in the mud,
then jumping in and going...

SPLAT!

"I'm worried if I have a bath,
you'll put an end to all of that."

The queen gave Grace a kiss
and then she hugged her very tight.

"You can squelch in mud
all day, if you'll just have
a bath each night!"

So the queen ran the **bubbliest** bath. The princess splished and **splashed** for hours.

Grace even enjoyed herself and smelled like sweet spring flowers.

Then as a special treat for Grace, her parents planned a big surprise.
When the princess went outside, she couldn't believe her eyes!

The royal gardens were transformed into a **muddy** water park!

Grace **whooshed** down slippery slides and flumes all day till it got dark.

**Squelching** in the mud
was the most fun she'd ever had.

Then from that day on,
she thought baths **maybe**
weren't so bad.